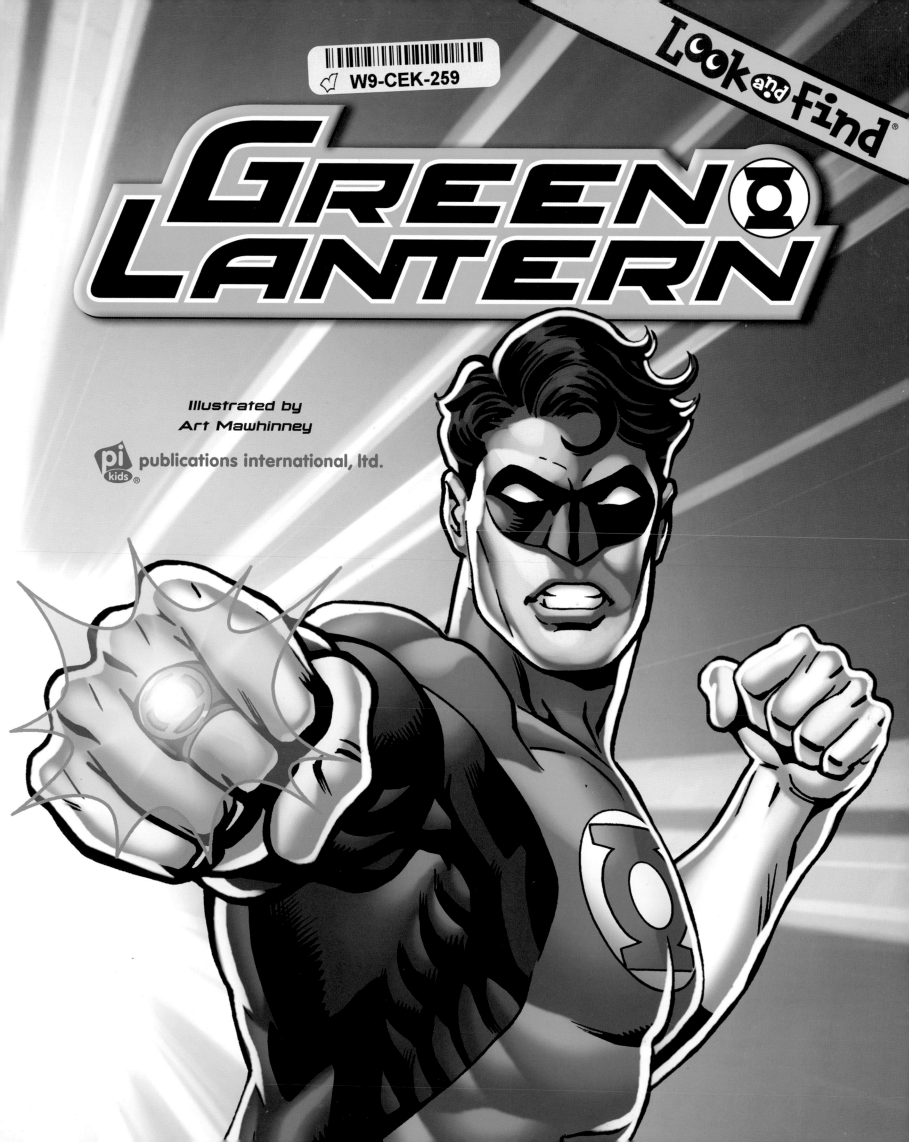

Hal

Arden

Carl Ferris

Laminski

Tom Kamalku

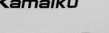
Carol Ferris

My name's Hal Jordan. I'm a pilot. At least, I used to be. I'm a mechanic here at Arden Airfield, but I'd give anything to fly again. Can you spot me working? What about these other people here?

The strangest thing just happened. I found myself here at this crashed ship ... an alien ship. Now Abin Sur is telling me I'm Earth's new Green Lantern. While I figure out what that means, see if you can find these things that the alien told me I'll need.

Power ring

Map showing Oa

Green Lantern symbol

Disguise

Power battery

Book of Oa

I was sent to the planet Oa, home of the Green Lantern Corps and the Guardians of the Universe. What a strange place. I'm supposed to find some of my fellow Lanterns before I report to boot camp. Do you see them?

B'dg

Ke'Haan

Kilowog

Arisia

Boodikka

G'nort

Tomar-Re

This is Ringslingin' 101, as Kilowog calls it. Some of it reminds me of my military days ... and some of it is very different. While I learn the ropes, see if you can spot me, along with these other Green Lanterns completing their training.

I've had all sorts of adventures as the Green Lantern. I even battled a mutant shark creature. He was tough, but I was tougher. With my ring, I can create constructs that look like anything I desire ... I just imagine them and they become real. Do you see these?

Harpoon

Electric eels

Stinging ray

Torpedo

Angry school of fish

Pinching crab

Sinestro and his corps of Yellow Lanterns once launched an attack against us. Those guys will stop at nothing to get what they want. Good thing we Green Lanterns stick together. Can you figure out who's who in this epic space battle?

Arisia

Hal Jordan

Lyssa Drak

Sinestro

Kilowog

Anti-Monitor

Just when I thought Earth was safe for a while, the Manhunters – deadly robots – decided to pay a visit to my hometown. Lucky for Coast City, help is never far away. As I fight to save the city – and Earth – look around for these Manhunters my Green Lantern friends are defeating.

In brightest day, in blackest night, no evil shall escape my sight. Let those who worship evil's might beware my power: Green Lantern's light!

Green Lanterns have an important job. The order of the universe rests on our shoulders. Becoming a Green Lantern changed my life...but I wouldn't have it any other way. Look around for me and some of my fellow Green Lanterns who have taken the sacred oath.

Guy Gardner

Hal Jordan

Kyle Rayner

John Stewart

Tomar-Re

Arisia

Kilowog

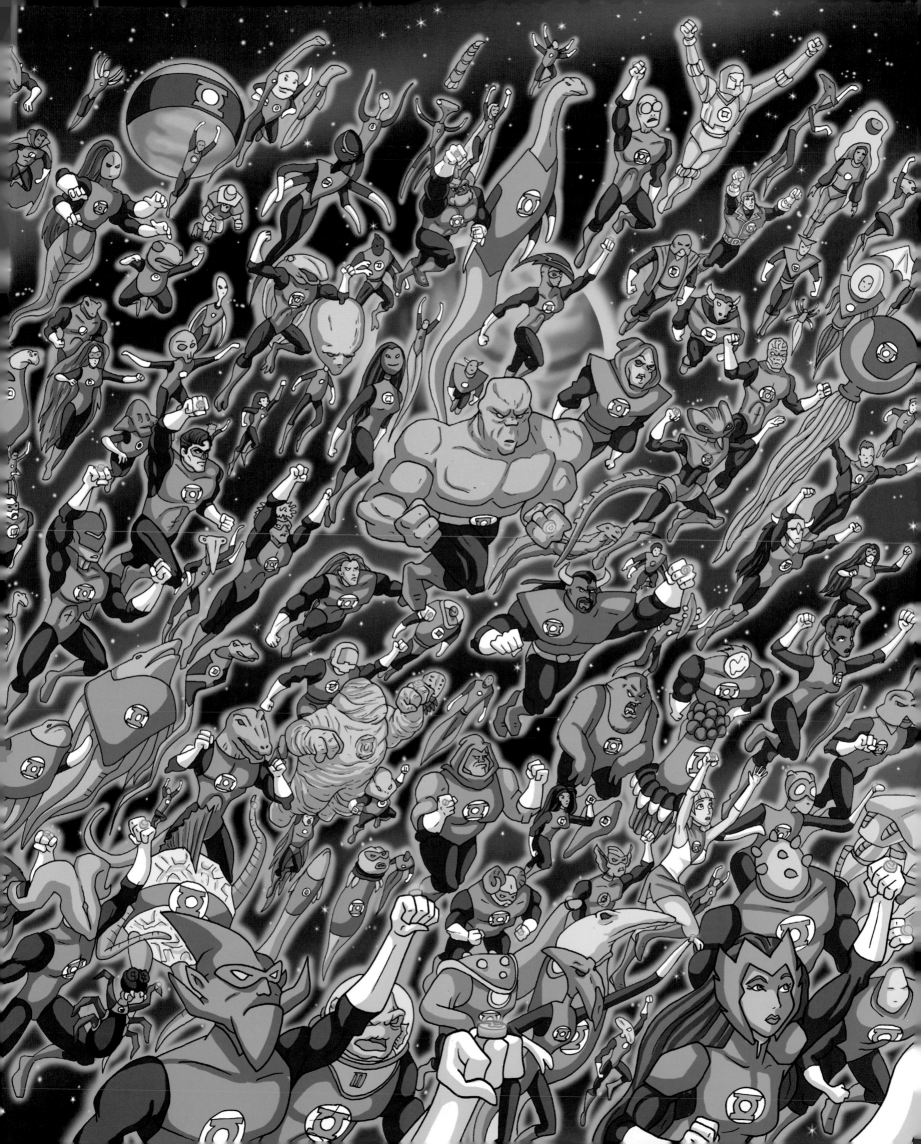

Zoom back to the crash site and look for these ship parts scattered among the debris.

Fly back to Arden Airfield and look for some mementos from Hal's past.

 Photo with his dad

His dad's jacket

His brother Jim's gift

Flight suit

 Model airplane

 Photo of his mom

Helmet

Flight journal

Run back to Ringslingin' 101 and count 36 yellow discs Kilowog is using to train the corps.

Oa is run by 12 all-knowing Guardians of the Universe. Power back to Oa and see if you can find all 12.

Dive back into the underwater battle and search for these other kinds of sharks.

Hammerhead shark

Great white shark

Reef shark

Whale shark

Bull shark

Tiger shark

Megamouth shark

Fight your way back to the space battle and look for these animal-inspired constructs both sides are using.

Cockroach

Serpent

Shark

Sabretooth tiger

Fanged horse

Dragon

Crocodile

Make your way back to Coast City and find these fearless residents helping the Green Lanterns save their city.

Soar back into space and look for a few more Green Lanterns who have taken the sacred oath.

Lysandra

Ash-Pak-Glif

Apros

Matoo and Amnee Pree

Norchavius

Mogo